Dear Parent:

Congratulations! Your child is taking the first steps on an exciting journey. The destination? Independent reading!

STEP INTO READING® will help your child get there. The program offers books at five levels that accompany children from their first attempts at reading to reading success. Each step includes fun stories, fiction and nonfiction, and colorful art. There are also Step into Reading Sticker Books, Step into Reading Math Readers, and Step into Reading Phonics Readers—a complete literacy program with something to interest every child.

Learning to Read, Step by Step!

Ready to Read Preschool–Kindergarten
• big type and easy words • rhyme and rhythm • picture clues
For children who know the alphabet and are eager to begin reading.

Reading with Help Preschool–Grade 1
• basic vocabulary • short sentences • simple stories
For children who recognize familiar words and sound out new words with help.

Reading on Your Own Grades 1–3
• engaging characters • easy-to-follow plots • popular topics
For children who are ready to read on their own.

Reading Paragraphs Grades 2–3
• challenging vocabulary • short paragraphs • exciting stories
For newly independent readers who read simple sentences with confidence.

Ready for Chapters Grades 2–4
• chapters • longer paragraphs • full-color art
For children who want to take the plunge into chapter books but still like colorful pictures.

STEP INTO READING® is designed to give every child a successful reading experience. The grade levels are only guides. Children can progress through the steps at their own speed, developing confidence in their reading, no matter what their grade.

Remember, a lifetime love of reading starts with a single step!

 Published in the United States by Random House Children's Books, a division of Random House, Inc., New York, and simultaneously in Canada by Random House of Canada Limited, Toronto.

www.stepintoreading.com
www.berenstainbears.com

Educators and librarians, for a variety of teaching tools, visit us at www.randomhouse.com/teachers

Library of Congress Cataloging-in-Publication Data
Berenstain, Stan, 1923–
The Berenstain Bears and the tic-tac-toe mystery / The Berenstains.
p. cm. — (Step into reading. A step 3 book.)
SUMMARY: The Bear Detectives try to figure out how Tic-Tac-Tom always wins at tic-tac-toe and whether he is cheating.
ISBN 0-679-89229-X (trade) — ISBN 0-679-99229-4 (lib. bdg.)
[1. Bears—Fiction. 2. Tic-tac-toe—Fiction. 3. Cheating—Fiction. 4. Mystery and detective stories.]
I. Berenstain, Jan, 1923– . II. Title. III. Step into reading. Step 3 book.
PZ7.B4483Bekr 2003 [Fic]—dc21 2002013247

Printed in the United States of America 14 13 12 11 10 9

STEP INTO READING®

STEP 3

The Berenstain Bears AND THE TIC-TAC-TOE MYSTERY

The Berenstains

Random House New York

WANTED
D
D
D

I'm Brother Bear.
Sister Bear, Cousin Fred,
Lizzy Bruin, and I
are the Bear Detectives.
We solve mysteries.

Our office is
in a big hollow tree.
We share the hollow tree
with Dr. Wise Old Owl.
Sometimes we call him in
on *really* tough cases.

One day, when we were waiting
for our next case to come along,
it walked right in the door.
"We need help," said Little Len.
Little Len was a cub
from down the road.

“Who’s *we*?” asked Sister.

“My friends and I,”

said Little Len.

“What seems to be the problem?”

asked Cousin Fred.

“Well, it’s like this,”
said Little Len.
“My friends and I play
a lot of tic-tac-toe.
We enjoy playing tic-tac-toe.
At least, we enjoyed it
until Tic-Tac-Tom came along.
Now we don’t enjoy it at all.”

TIC·TAC

TIC·TAC·TOM
THE WORLD'S
GREATEST
TIC·TAC·TOE
PLAYER
TIC·TAC·TOM
THE WORLD'S
GREATEST
TIC·TAC·TOE
PLAYER

"Why is that?" asked Lizzy.

"Because," said Little Len,

"Tic-Tac-Tom wins every time.

And when he wins,

he hoots and hollers.

He jumps up and down

and shouts,

'I won! I won!

I'm the best! I'm the best!'"

“That’s not very good
sportsmanship,” said Sister.
“But maybe he wins
because he’s the best player.”
“That isn’t the worst of it,”
continued Little Len.

"He wears a shirt that says

TIC-TAC-TOM,

THE WORLD'S GREATEST

TIC-TAC-TOE PLAYER!"

The shirt did it.

The Bear Detectives

took the case.

Little Len took us to the place
where Tic-Tac-Tom played
his tic-tac-toe games.
We studied the scene.
We studied Tic-Tac-Tom.

D
D
PLAYE

It was just
as Little Len had said:
Tic-Tac-Tom
took on all comers
and won every single game.

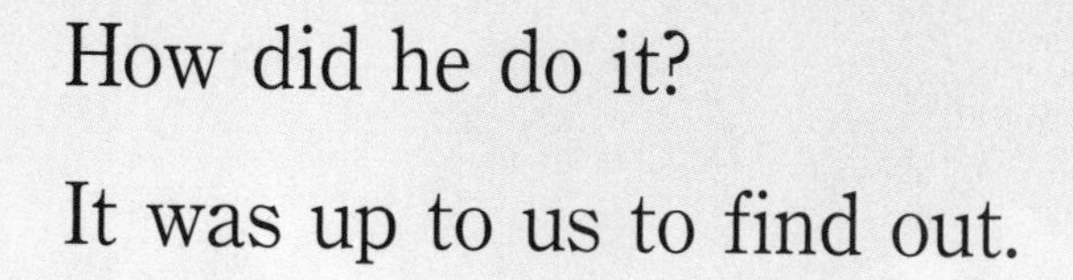

How did he do it?

It was up to us to find out.

"Hmm," said Sister
as Tic-Tac-Tom hooted
and hollered after every win.
"Hmm," said Fred.
"I used to play tic-tac-toe
when I was younger.
It seems to me
that the player who goes first
almost always wins."

TIC·TAC·TOM
THE WORLD'S
GREATEST
TIC·TAC·TOE
PLAYER

TIC·TAC·TOM
THE WORLD'S
GREATEST
TIC·TAC·TOE
PLAYER

"Hmm," said Lizzy
as Tic-Tac-Tom tossed a coin
to see who would go first.
"What could be fairer
than that?" she asked.
I didn't have an answer,
but something told me
that something fishy
was going on.

Maybe it was
the hooting
and hollering.

Maybe it was
the jumping up and down.

Maybe it was the shirt.
But whatever it was,

I decided to
make my move.

THE WORLD'S
GREATEST
TIC·TAC·TOM
THE WORLD'S
GREATEST
TIC·TAC·TOE
PLAYER

I told my fellow detectives
that I was going to challenge
Tic-Tac-Tom to a game.
"And while I'm playing him,"
I said,
"you watch his every move."

"Hi there, Tic-Tac-Tom," I said.
"Let's play a game."
"Don't mind if I do,"
said Tic-Tac-Tom.

My partners watched like hawks
as Tom drew a tic-tac-toe grid.
It looked like a perfectly good grid
to the Bear Detectives.

My partners watched like hawks
as Tom tossed a coin
to see who would go first.

"Heads, I win. Tails, you lose,"
said Tom as he tossed the coin.
Tom won the toss and went first.
But what could be fairer
than that?

HEADS, I WIN. TAILS, YOU LOSE.
TIC·TAC·TOM
THE WORLD'S GREATEST TIC·TAC·TOE PLAYER

My partners watched like hawks
as Tom gave me my choice
of X's or O's.
I chose O's.

But then it was

zip-zip-zap, zip-zip-zap,

and it was all over.

Tic-Tac-Tom had won

another game of tic-tac-toe.

How had he done it?

I huddled with
my fellow detectives.
"Well," I said,
"what do you think?"
"We don't know what to think,"
said Fred.
"Maybe it's a trick coin," said Lizzy.
"No," I said.
"It was a proper coin,
with a head on one side
and a tail on the other."

"This is a toughie,"
said Sister with a sigh.
"I sure wish Dr. Wise Old Owl
was here to help us."
Dr. Wise Old Owl *was* there,
and he'd been watching
like an owl.
"Whooo!" he said.
"Look!" cried Sister.
"It's Dr. Wise Old Owl!
Can you help us
solve the mystery
of Tic-Tac-Tom's winning ways?"

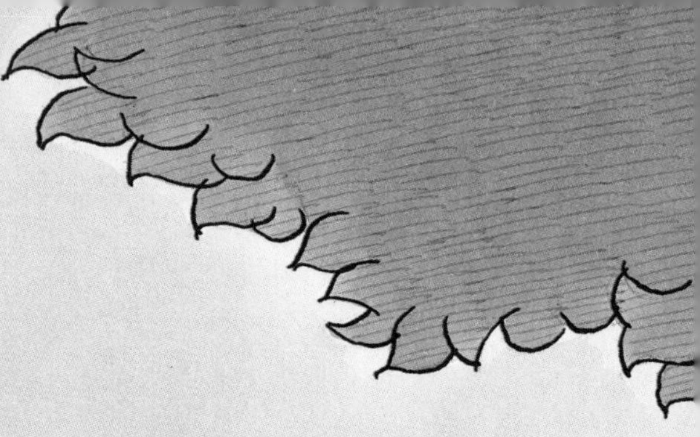

This is what Dr. Wise Old Owl said:

"Take some advice
from a wise old bird.
When Tom tosses the coin,
study each and every word."

"When Tom tosses the coin,"
repeated Fred,
"study each and every word."

Tom had finished hooting
and hollering over his win.
He was just about
to toss the coin
for his next game.

The Bear Detectives
studied each and every word
as Tom tossed the coin and said,
“Heads, I win. Tails, you lose.”

"That's it!" I cried.
"Tic-Tac-Tom,
your tic-tac-toe-winning days
are over!"

“I don’t get it,” said Little Len.

“Why are his winning days over?”

“Because,” I explained,

“‘Heads, I win. Tails, you lose’

is a trick.

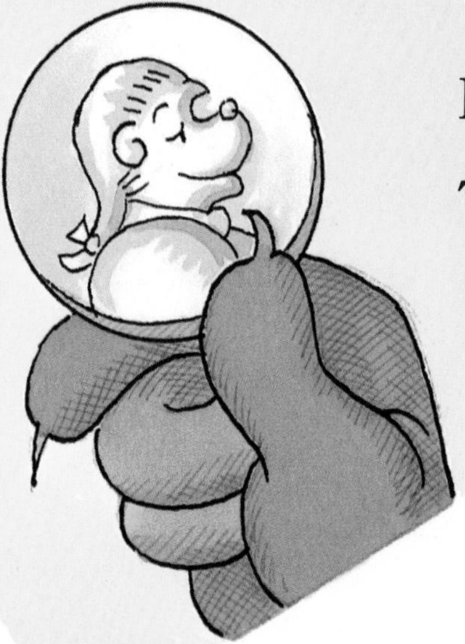

If it's heads,
Tom goes first.

If it's tails,
Tom goes first
just the same.

He should say,
'Heads, I win. Tails, you win'!"

Little Len and his friends
still play tic-tac-toe a lot.
They even let Tom play sometimes.
But now everybody
has a chance to win.

And the Bear Detectives have
had the satisfaction
of solving another mystery—

with a little help from a friend,

of course.

SSI

STRATEGIC STUDIES INSTITUTE

AFTER IRAQ:

The Search for a Sustainable National Security Strategy

Colin S. Gray

STRATEGIC STUDIES INSTITUTE

The Strategic Studies Institute (SSI) is part of the U.S. Army War College and is the strategic level study agent for issues related to national security and military strategy with emphasis on geostrategic analysis.

The mission of SSI is to use independent analysis to conduct strategic studies that develop policy recommendations on:

- Strategy, planning and policy for joint and combined employment of military forces;
- Regional strategic appraisals;
- The nature of land warfare;
- Matters affecting the Army's future;
- The concepts, philosophy, and theory of strategy; and
- Other issues of importance to the leadership of the Army.

Studies produced by civilian and military analysts concern topics having strategic implications for the Army, the Department of Defense, and the larger national security community.

In addition to its studies, SSI publishes special reports on topics of special or immediate interest. These include edited proceedings of conferences and topically-orientated roundtables, expanded trip reports, and quick reaction responses to senior Army leaders.

The Institute provides a valuable analytical capability within the Army to address strategic and other issues in support of Army participation in national security policy formulation.